The Pink Panther and the Fancy Party

by SANDRA BERIS

illustrated by DARRELL BAKER

GOLDEN PRESS • NEW YORK

Western Publishing Company, Inc., Racine, Wisconsin

Copyright © 1983 by United Artists. All rights reserved. Printed in the U.S.A. by Western Publishing Company, Inc. No part of this book may be reproduced or copied in any form without written permission from the publisher. Golden® A Golden Look-Look® Book, and Golden Press® are trademarks of Western Publishing Company, Inc. Library of Congress Catalog Card Number 82-82613 ISBN 0-307-11887-8

A B C D E F G H I J

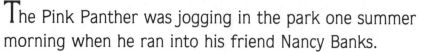

The Pink Panther was jogging in the park one summer morning when he ran into his friend Nancy Banks.

"You're just the panther I wanted to see!" said Nancy. "Can you come to my birthday party? It's on Friday at four o'clock."

"Splendid!" said the Pink Panther.

"It's going to be a fancy party," said Nancy. "Be sure to dress up."

"I'll be the fanciest fellow there," said the Pink Panther.

On the day of the party, the Pink Panther hurried down the street toward Nancy's house. He was very pleased with his present for Nancy—a bright pink parasol.

Along the way he stopped to look at his reflection in a store window. "Tsk, tsk," he said to himself. "I don't look fancy enough for the party. I should have worn a hat. My tie should be brighter."

The Pink Panther scooted into a small clothing store and told the salesman he wanted to look at hats and ties.

The salesman glanced at his watch nervously. "Well, only if it's a *quick* look," he said. "I have to close early today."

"I'll be especially speedy," the Pink Panther promised.

First the Pink Panther looked at hats. He tried on a big cowboy hat, but it was too wild for Nancy's party.

Then he tried on a small cap, but it was too plain.

He tried on a black top hat, but it was too dressy.

Finally the Pink Panther spotted a straw boater. "Aha!" he cried. "Now *that's* a fancy hat!" He admired it from the front...

and from the side.

He tossed it gracefully in the air and...

... caught it with the pink parasol.

"You've punched a hole in the hat!" said the salesman angrily.
"Oops," said the Pink Panther. "Well, look on the bright side.
Now the hat is *air-conditioned!*"
"It's ruined!" shouted the salesman. "You'll have to pay for it."

"Not to worry, said the Pink Panther, giving the salesman some money. "Let's forget about hats," he went on. "What I really need is a fancy tie."

"Just hurry," said the salesman. "I *have* to close."

The Pink Panther raced to the nearest tie rack. In his rush, he tossed ties left and right.

"Stop!" cried the salesman. "You're messing up the store!"

At that moment, the Pink Panther found a tie he liked. "Perfect!" he said. "I'll try it on."

"Just buy it and leave," pleaded the salesman. But the Pink Panther put on the tie, swirled and twirled in front of the mirror, until suddenly—

CRASH! The tie display fell to the floor. The salesman groaned and began picking up ties.

"Let me help," said the Pink Panther politely.

"NO!" screamed the salesman. "Just go away!"

"Precisely what I had planned," answered the Pink Panther.

But on his way out of the store, the Pink Panther saw another rack of ties—very colorful ones. "I *must* look at these," he said to the salesman. "This time I'll try them on *you*. That way I won't knock anything over."

The salesman sighed helplessly.

Soon the salesman was covered with ties. A certain pink and green silk one on the salesman's right arm pleased the Pink Panther the most. He looked at the tie closely.

"I'll be a panther's uncle!" he cried. "That's the tie I was wearing when I came in!"

The exhausted salesman said nothing.

"Speechless, eh?" said the Pink Panther. "Well, I'll trouble you no longer. Thanks for everything. Good-bye!"

As soon as the Pink Panther left the store, the salesman locked the doors and hobbled quickly to his car.

The Pink Panther hummed a happy tune as he walked down the street. "How do you like that," he said to himself. "I had the fanciest tie to begin with!"

Soon the Pink Panther arrived at Nancy's house. The guests were gathered around the pool in the back yard. The Pink Panther said hello to Mrs. Banks and then presented his gift to Nancy.

"A little something for the birthday girl," he said with a bow.

"Oh thank you," said Nancy. Then she added, "Pink Panther, you look handsome today."

"Come and meet my father," said Nancy. "But be very nice to him. He had a bad day at work."

"Leave it to me," said the Pink Panther. "No one can cheer people up faster than a Pink Panther."

But when the Pink Panther saw Nancy's father, he stopped in his tracks. Nancy's father was the salesman from the clothing store!

When Mr. Banks saw the Pink Panther, he jumped out of his chair and staggered backward. "Keep that pink peril away from me!" he screamed.

"Watch out, Mr. Banks!" said the Pink Panther.

"Watch out, Daddy!" said Nancy.

But it was too late.

SPLASH! Nancy's father fell into the pool. Water flew
everywhere. The Pink Panther put up Nancy's parasol just in time.
"I always give practical presents," he said to her with a smile.

Nancy's father climbed out of the pool, growling like a bear. He headed straight for the Pink Panther.

"Now it's *your* turn for a swim, Pinky," he said.

The Pink Panther gulped. "It's a fine day for a dip," he said, "but I didn't bring my suit."

"I can't seem to dress correctly today," the Pink Panther said to himself as he ran across the lawn. "The way things have turned out, I should have worn my jogging clothes!"